DATE DUE

For you both with my love

Sharing

NANETTE NEWMAN
Illustrated by Liz Moyes

DOUBLEDAY
NEW YORK   LONDON   TORONTO   SYDNEY   AUCKLAND

"Do you know what?" asked Amy's mommy.

"What?" asked Amy.

"I've got a baby in my tummy."

"Why?" asked Amy.

"Well," said her mommy, "I thought it would be nice for you to have a brother or a sister."

Amy thought for a minute.

"Could you have a dog instead?" she asked.

"Now, don't be silly," said her mommy. "Would you like to feel it?"

Amy put her hands on her mommy's tummy.

"There—did you feel it kick?" asked her mommy.

"Why don't you give it a smack?" asked Amy.

Her mommy pulled down her sweater and told Amy it was time to go to the park.

Amy sat in the sandbox with her friend Cleo.

"My mommy's got a baby in her tummy," said Amy.

"Oh," said Cleo. "When will it come out?"

"When it feels like it," said Amy.

"Will it be a boy baby or a girl?" asked Cleo.

"No one knows," said Amy.

"Do you wish it was a dog?" asked Cleo.

"Yes," said Amy.

The time went by, and Amy's mommy's tummy
grew bigger. . .

and bigger.

One day when Amy was eating her boiled egg
and toast, she asked her mommy, "If we don't
like this baby, can we put it back?"

"No, silly," said her mommy. "Besides, I **know**
you'll like it; it will be a friend for you. A friend
who will be with you forever."

Amy turned her egg upside down and hit it
with her spoon.

At the end of the summer, when the sandbox
had been put away and all the leaves were falling
off the trees, Amy's mommy showed her the new
crib.

Amy got in it one day—with the cat from next door.

Her mommy said she'd rather she didn't do that any more, and bought her a toy crib for her doll Gus, but Gus didn't like it and went back to sleeping in Amy's bed.

"Wouldn't it be exciting if our baby was here in time for Christmas?" asked Daddy when they were putting decorations on the Christmas tree.

"Will it try and open my stocking?" asked Amy.

"Of course not," said Daddy. "It'll be too little."

Amy stared at the angel on top of the Christmas tree and made a wish.

Soon after Christmas Day when Santa Claus had come and gone and Amy and Cleo had played with each other's presents, Daddy came rushing in and said, "I've got a great surprise for you."

Amy looked up from her painting, hoping it was a dog. "The baby has just come out of mommy's tummy, and if you're very quiet we can go and take a look."

Amy looked at the baby.

"What do you think?" asked her mommy.
"Where's the rest of it?" asked Amy.

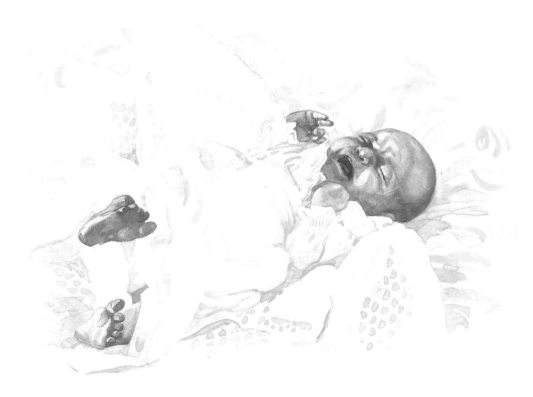

Her mommy unwrapped the blanket and there
was the baby not much bigger than Amy's doll
Gus.

"It's a little boy," said mommy. "And we'll call
him Ben. Ben, this is your sister, Amy Rose."

"What's he like?" asked Cleo.

"Squashed up," said Amy. "All he does is drink mommy's milk, and go to the bathroom."

"He sounds silly," said Cleo.

"He is," said Amy.

"When will he play with us?" asked Cleo.

"His feet have got to grow a bit first," said Amy.

All through the spring Ben was busy growing. Sometimes Amy gave him a bottle, but he was very squirmy. She tried to help bathe him, but he was very slippery.

In the summer Ben was given a teddy bear that Amy liked a lot—so she took it away from him.

"Now, that's not very nice," said Daddy. "You must always remember about sharing."

Amy wished some days that **she** was a baby.
In fact, some days she pretended she **was** a baby
—she spat her food out,

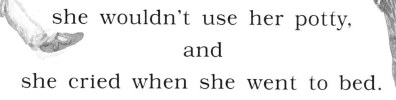

she wouldn't use her potty,
and
she cried when she went to bed.

"You're being silly," said her mommy.

"I'm not," said Amy. "I want to be a baby."

"But you were a baby," said mommy, "and now you're my special big girl—and Ben's the baby."

On the morning of Ben's first birthday, Amy sat beside him in her new party dress for a photograph.

He had a cake with one candle.

"What do you think he'd like for his birthday?" asked mommy.

"He wants a dog," said Amy.

But he didn't get one. He got some toy bricks instead.

Soon Amy started going to nursery school in the mornings. She went with her friend Cleo, and they did finger painting and singing and made things out of colored paper. Amy could count up to twenty.

"You can't do that, can you, Ben?" asked Amy.

"Yes," said Ben.

"Don't be silly," said Amy.

When Amy came home from school, Ben would get very excited and dribble and try to walk and fall down a lot. He would shout, "Mamie!"

Sometimes he'd been playing with Amy's toys while she'd been at school.

"Bad boy, Ben," she'd say, and one day she gave him a pinch.

Big tears fell out of his eyes, and he started to cry.

Amy's mommy shouted from the kitchen, "What's going on?"

"Nothing!" shouted Amy.

"Why did you do it?" asked Cleo.

"I don't know," said Amy.

When Ben could walk he wanted to go everywhere with Amy. Sometimes she'd let him, and sometimes she wouldn't.

They slept in the same room now, and in the morning Amy would look out of her bed and see Ben, and Ben would look out of his bed and see Amy.

One day Ben started playing
with Gus, so

Amy snatched Gus away—

Ben snatched him back,
and then Amy pushed Ben,
and Ben pushed Amy.

"It's mine!" shouted Amy.
"It's mine!" shouted Ben.
He'd learned to talk now.

In November Amy had a bad cold. Her head felt hot and her nose felt stuffy. She had to stay in bed.

Ben came and sat beside her. He brought her all his books, his new toy car, and his favorite teddy bear.

When Amy was better, Mommy took her and Ben to the playground for a treat. Lots of children were there—Cleo was on the swings and another girl named Lucy was on the slide.

Ben loved the slide.

Suddenly Amy saw Lucy push Ben over.

"It's *my* slide!" she was shouting. "You can't have a turn!"

When Amy saw Lucy push Ben again, she rushed over to his side. She helped him up—his knee was bleeding, but he was being very brave. Amy put her arm around him.

"He's only little—don't you ever do that again," she said.

"Why not?" asked Lucy.

"Because he's my brother, and I love him, and I won't let anybody hurt him."

On the day that school finished for the
Christmas holidays, Amy and Cleo were sitting
on the steps eating a peanut butter sandwich.

"I'm getting a dog for Christmas," said Cleo.

"Oh," said Amy, taking a big bite.

"Will you be sad you don't have one?" asked
Cleo.

Amy thought. "Oh no," she said. "I'd much rather have a brother."

And she meant it.

Published by Doubleday, a division of
Bantam Doubleday Dell Publishing Group, Inc.
666 Fifth Avenue, New York, New York 10103

Doubleday and the portrayal of an anchor
with a dolphin are trademarks of
Doubleday, a division of Bantam Doubleday Dell
Publishing Group, Inc.

Library of Congress Cataloging-in-Publication Data
Newman, Nanette.
Sharing/Nanette Newman; illustrated by Liz Moyes.
p.   cm.
Summary: Amy feels threatened by the arrival of her new baby
brother, Ben, but after acting out her resentment, she learns how
wonderful being a big sister can be.
[1. Brothers and sisters—Fiction.   2. Babies—Fiction.]
I. Moyes, Liz, ill.   II. Title.
PZ7.N4853Sh   1990
[E]—dc20   89-34539   CIP   AC

ISBN 0-385-41104-9
ISBN 0-385-41105-7 (lib. bdg.)
Text copyright © 1989 by Bryan Forbes Ltd.
Illustrations copyright © 1989 by Liz Moyes